STO

FRIENDS
OF ACPL

jE
Barber, Barbara E.
Saturday at the new you

3/95

W9-DDA-141

ALLEN COUNTY PUBLIC LIBRARY

FORT WAYNE, INDIANA 46802

You may return this book to any location of
the Allen County Public Library.

DEMCO

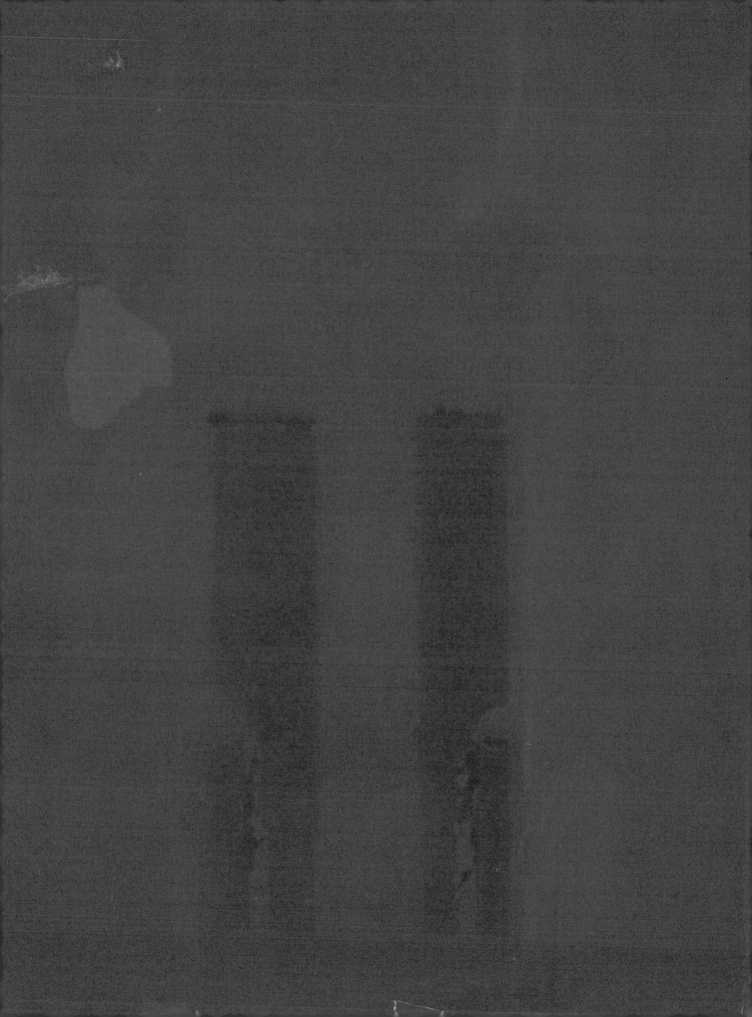

SATURDAY
AT
The New You

by Barbara E. Barber

Illustrated by Anna Rich

LEE & LOW BOOKS Inc. • New York

Text copyright © 1994 by Barbara E. Barber
Illustrations copyright © 1994 by Anna Rich
All rights reserved. No part of the contents of this book may be
reproduced by any means without the written permission of the publisher.
LEE & LOW BOOKS Inc., 228 East 45th Street, New York, NY 10017

Printed in Hong Kong by South China Printing Co. (1988) Ltd.

Book Design by Christy Hale
Book Production by Our House

The text is set in Impressum Bold
The illustrations are rendered in oil paint on canvas.
10 9 8 7 6 5 4 3 2 1
First Edition

Library of Congress Cataloguing-in-Publication Data
Barber, Barbara E.,
Saturday at The New New/by Barbara E. Barber;
illustrated by Anna Rich. — First ed.
p. cm.
Summary: Shauna, a young African American girl,
wishes she could do more to help Momma with the customers
at her beauty salon. Then one day she gets her chance.
ISBN 1-880000-06-7 (hardcover)
[1. Afro-Americans—Fiction. 2. Mothers and daughters—Fiction.
3. Beauty shops—Fiction.]
I. Rich, Anna, ill. II. Title.
PZ7.B2326Sat 1994
[E]—dc20   93-5165
CIP AC

To my mother, Rosalie Smith,
a little woman with a lot of endurance;
and to the memory of my father, Johnny Smith

—B.E.B.

Thanks to Karina O. and Saskia K.
for their invaluable assistance,
and to Liz Szabla for her exemplary stamina

—A.R.

Saturday is my favorite day of the week. Saturday is when
I help Momma in her beauty parlor across the street from our
apartment. It's called The New You.

On Saturdays Daddy walks us to The New You and helps us lift the metal gate. Then he kisses me and Momma good-bye and goes to work downtown. Saturday is a day for me and Momma.

As soon as we unlock the door and walk inside The New You, Momma turns on the lights. The pink hair dryers look so shiny you almost have to squint. The New You has pictures on the wall with lots of different hairstyles. Long hair, short hair, natural hair, straight hair, curly hair; Momma says all hair is beautiful.

While Momma hangs up her coat, I jump in a chair and spin round and round and make funny faces in the mirror until I get dizzy.

"Shauna, I see you making those silly faces!" Momma yells. "One day you're going to make a face and it'll stick."

"Aw, Momma." I've made funny faces a million times.

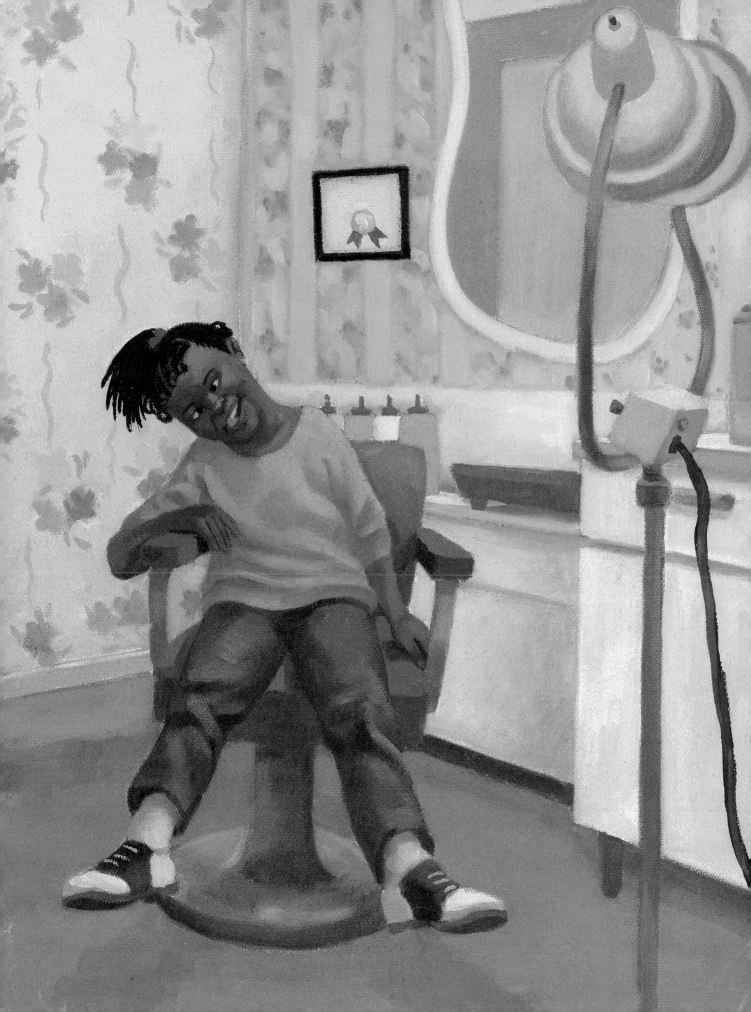

Momma turns on the music after the lights. She says she works better to music, and The New You is always full of rhythm. As Momma stacks the clean towels near the sink, I hold a brush in my hands like a microphone and pretend I'm a famous singer. I sit my dolls, Stacey and Kenya, up on the counter so they can see my performance. Even though Momma says that I make too much noise in the morning, I can usually hear her humming to the music, too.

Before I'm done with my first song, Momma calls me to the back room so I can put on my smock. Momma made us special smocks with flowers. Mine says *Shauna* in red fancy letters.

We make coffee for the customers who come early. I get to arrange the packets of sugar while Momma measures the coffee. The New You smells so good on Saturday mornings—like sweet peach shampoo and strawberry conditioner and fresh coffee.

Today Momma's first customer won't be having coffee, though. Her name is Tiffany Peters. Tiffany lives in my building, and she just turned five. She always has her thumb in her mouth and a scowl on her face. She never likes anything, not the candy Momma offers, or the magazines I show her, or the hairstyle Momma gives her.

"Shauna, please hand me the brush and the towel over there," Momma says, pointing to the counter closest to me. Little Tiffany has to pop her thumb out of her mouth when Momma puts the smock over her head. I watch Momma brush out Tiffany's curly hair until it's fluffy as a cloud.

"I can do that," I tell Momma as I watch her rub conditioner through Tiffany's hair after she's washed it. Momma uses the same conditioner on me, and it makes my hair soft and shiny. It smells nice, too. My favorite is the one that smells like coconuts.

Momma's humming along with the music and I don't think she hears me, so I tell her again.

"I can do that!"

"Maybe you can." Momma smiles. "But Tiffany is *my* customer."

"Yeah," Tiffany says. She takes her thumb out of her mouth long enough to stick her tongue out at me. She can sure act like a baby!

3 1833 02634 0494

While Tiffany and Mrs. Peters let the conditioner sit, Momma starts helping her other customers. Pretty soon The New You is crowded with people getting their hair washed and dried, cut and styled, combed and brushed. One of my jobs is to bring customers magazines while they wait for Momma. Sometimes their friends pass by on the street and wave or come inside to visit.

I watch Momma press Ms. Escobar's hair with a hot comb and curl it with a curling iron. Ms. Escobar is one of Momma's regular customers, and she's a teacher at my school. When Momma's done curling, she combs and twists and pins Ms. Escobar's red hair on top of her head. I'm thinking about fixing Stacey's hair the very same way when Ms. Escobar catches me staring at her.

"Well?" she asks, smiling. I smile back. I've never seen her yell at any of the kids at school, even the hard-headed ones. "What do you think?"

"Gorgeous," I tell her, pretending she's *my* customer. "It's a new you!" I say, just like Momma. I hope I get to be in Ms. Escobar's class when I start third grade.

Mrs. Johnson walks in carrying a box from her bakery down the block. I love her jelly doughnuts and chocolate chip cookies and sweet potato pies. Her shop is always busy, just like Momma's.

After Momma puts rollers in Mrs. Johnson's hair, it's time to sit under the dryer. I hate sitting under the dryer; it's hot and noisy and you can't move. It's so boring! But Mrs. Johnson doesn't think so.

"I look forward to my Saturdays under the dryer," she tells me. "It's the only time I can take a nap without being disturbed." When Mrs. Johnson takes a nap under the dryer, all you can see is her wide-open mouth. She snores real loud. But you can't hear her snoring when the dryer's on.

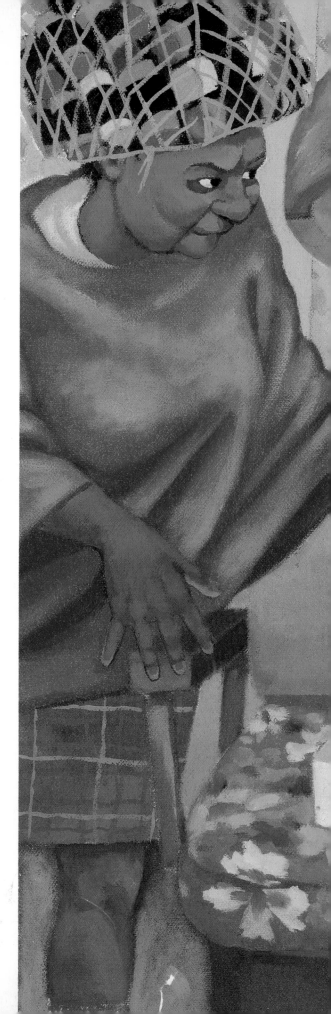

After the dryer turns off, Momma takes the rollers out of Mrs. Johnson's hair. I wish I could style Mrs. Johnson's hair, but all I do is put the rollers in a tray.

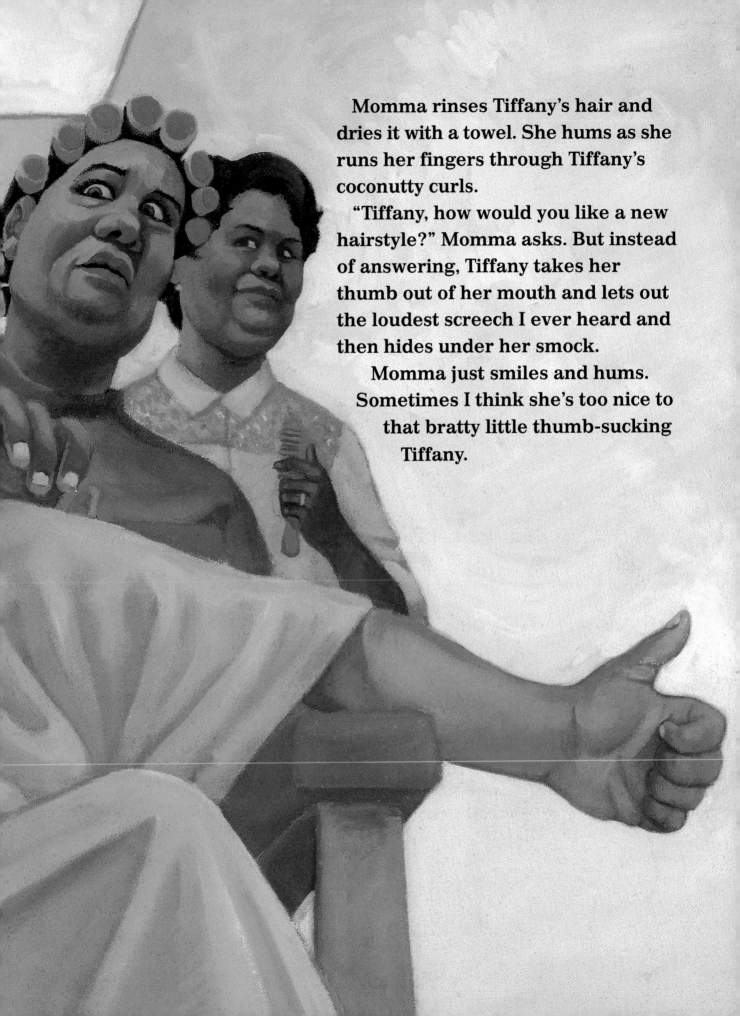

Momma rinses Tiffany's hair and dries it with a towel. She hums as she runs her fingers through Tiffany's coconutty curls.

"Tiffany, how would you like a new hairstyle?" Momma asks. But instead of answering, Tiffany takes her thumb out of her mouth and lets out the loudest screech I ever heard and then hides under her smock.

Momma just smiles and hums. Sometimes I think she's too nice to that bratty little thumb-sucking Tiffany.

I sit down with Kenya and
Stacey. Their hair looks a mess!
I take my Afro-comb and work
on Stacey's hair until it's nice
and full. I give her barrettes to
match her dress. I think Kenya's
hair looks good in braids, like
mine. I brush and braid a section
at a time until she has almost as
many braids as I do. I like it
when Momma puts beads in my
braids. But we don't have beads
small enough for Kenya, so I put
rubber bands at the tips of the
braids to keep them from
coming loose.

I walk over to Momma to show her what I've done.

"These are *my* customers," I say.

Momma feels Kenya's braids. I made them nice and tight. "Very good, Shauna!" she says. "What beautiful braids!"

"Hey!" Tiffany yells from her hiding place under the big smock. "I want braids, too!" She tries to uncover herself, but she's so small she just gets more tangled. Her mother helps her, and after a minute her little head pops out from the smock.

Momma trims Tiffany's hair and braids it so it looks a lot like Kenya's and mine. I sit on the counter in front of Tiffany and let her play with Stacey and Kenya. We eat some more of Mrs. Johnson's doughnuts and drink some juice while Momma finishes braiding.

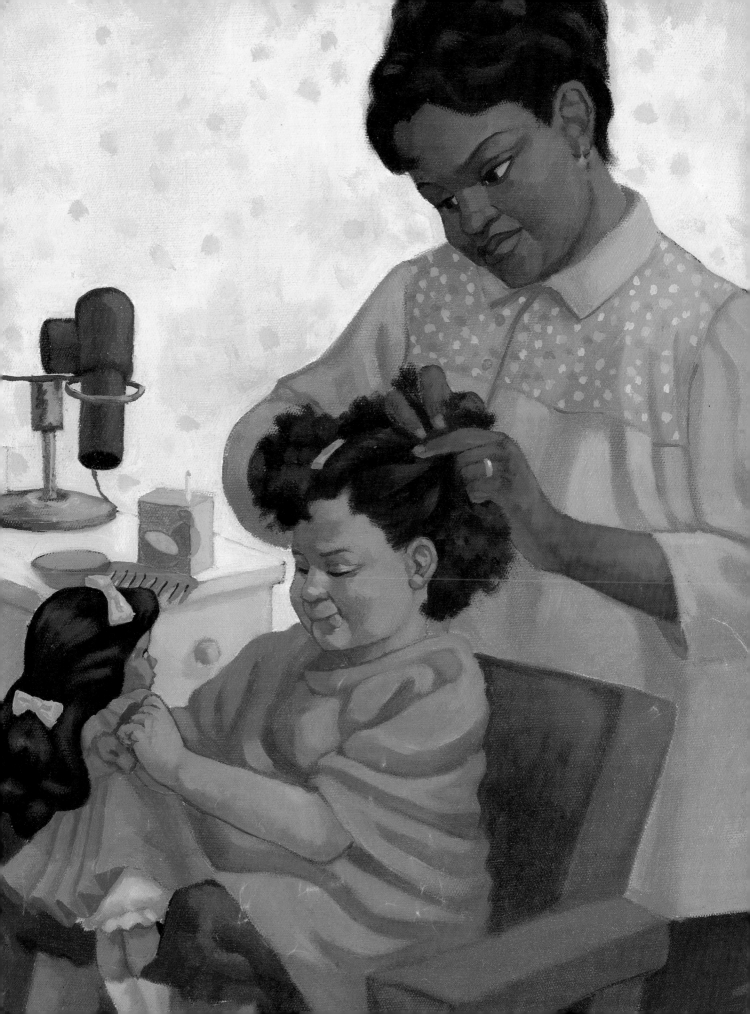

When Momma's done, I hop off the counter so Tiffany can see herself in the mirror.

"I look like a movie star!" she cries.

I hand her a mirror and show her how she can spin in her chair and see how her braids look in the back, just like Momma does with her customers.

"It's a new you!" I say.

"Thank you, Shauna," Momma and Mrs. Peters say at the same time.

By the time we're ready to close, Momma and I are exhausted from being on our feet all day. But Momma still sits me down in front of the mirror and fixes my braids and gives me a new clip to wear to Grandmomma and Granddaddy's house on Sunday.

"You're my favorite customer," Momma says. "And my favorite helper!"

Momma sits down by the window and starts to brush her own hair.

"I can do that!" I tell her. While I brush, Momma closes her eyes and hums along with the radio.